RANGER in TIME

Long Road to Freedom

P9-CAA-702

KATE MESSNER

illustrated by
KELLEY MCMORRIS

Scholastic Inc.

Text copyright © 2016 by Kate Messner
Illustrations copyright © 2016 by Scholastic Inc.

This book is being published simultaneously in hardcover by Scholastic Press.

Library of Congress Cataloging-in-Publication Data
Messner, Kate, author.
Long road to freedom / Kate Messner ; illustrated by Kelley McMorris.
pages cm. — (Ranger in time)
Summary: This time the mysterious box that Ranger the golden retriever found transports him to a Maryland plantation before the Civil War, where he must help a young house slave named Sarah and her younger brother, Jesse, find their way to the Underground Railroad and north to freedom, before Jesse is sold to a plantation further south.
1. Golden retriever — Juvenile fiction. 2. Underground Railroad — Juvenile fiction. 3. Time travel — Juvenile fiction. 4. Slavery — Maryland — Juvenile fiction. 5. African Americans — Maryland — Juvenile fiction. 6. Adventure stories. 7. Maryland — Juvenile fiction. [1. Golden retriever — Fiction. 2. Dogs — Fiction. 3. Underground Railroad — Fiction. 4. Time travel — Fiction. 5. Slavery — Fiction. 6. African Americans — Fiction. 7. Adventure and adventurers — Fiction. 8. Maryland — History — 1775–1865 — Fiction.] I. McMorris, Kelley, illustrator. II. Title. III. Series: Messner, Kate. Ranger in time.
PZ10.3.M5635Lo 2016
813.6 — dc23 2015006958

ISBN 978-0-545-63920-0

10 9 8 7 6 5 4 3 2   16 17 18 19 20

Printed in the United States of America   40
First printing 2016

Book design by Ellen Duda

For my editors, Cassandra and Anamika,
who help me find my way

**Special thanks to Dr. Raphael Rogers, EdD, at
Clark University for reading an early draft of
Long Road to Freedom *for historical accuracy
and providing invaluable feedback.***

Chapter 1

LAST CHANCE TO GO

Sarah hurried into the dining room with Master Bradley's breakfast, a plate piled with corn bread and cold ham. She set it on the table before him and stepped back against the wall to listen. All morning, the house had been full of buzz and chatter. That was never good.

The Bradleys had sold a dozen slaves this year because they'd switched from growing tobacco to mostly wheat on their tidewater Maryland plantation. Wheat wasn't as much work, so fewer slaves were needed. Simon and Moses and Henry — men Sarah had known her whole life — had already been sold south to work on a cotton plantation in Alabama.

"I can't imagine you'll get much for the boy. He's not strong enough." Mrs. Bradley set down her teacup and frowned at her husband.

Sarah's heart jumped into her throat. Were they talking about her brother, Jesse? There were other boys on the plantation, but Jesse was the youngest and smallest.

"Mr. Fenn will decide if he has value. We cannot afford to keep more than we need." Master Bradley wiped his mustache with his napkin and turned to Sarah. "Go up to the roof and watch for Mr. Fenn's boat. Come tell me when you see him approaching."

Sarah forced her voice to sound bored, as if she hadn't been paying attention to their conversation. "Yes, sir." She curtsied and hurried up to the third floor. She climbed the wooden ladder, unlatched the trapdoor, and pushed it open. A warm wind blew in off the creek.

Sarah climbed out onto the rooftop porch and looked over the fields to the water. All she saw was a fishing skiff and a bigger boat docked by the tobacco prize house. Old Isaac would be at the prizer now, using the machine to pack dried tobacco into hogsheads, getting ready to load the barrels onto the boat.

There was no sign of Mr. Fenn's schooner, which meant there was time to think. Time to learn more.

Sarah raced down the stairs and out the back door to the yew tree near the formal garden. William Bradley sat leaning against it with a book.

Sarah and William had been born the same week in April, twelve years ago. They'd played together as babies while Mama tended Mrs.

Bradley's kitchen garden. Both their mothers had gotten sick with fever three years ago. But only Mrs. Bradley had recovered.

Sarah was sad and quiet for a long time after her mama died. William tried to cheer her up with stories. He'd meet her after breakfast to share books from his tutor. One day, he started teaching her letters, and then words. Most slaves couldn't read, but the Bradleys didn't seem to mind if Sarah learned. She could read almost anything now.

But today, she had no interest in books. "Who's your father selling?"

William shrugged. "I don't know. But not you. That much is certain. You're my favorite."

"What about Jesse?"

"Father would never sell your brother," William said. But he looked away when he said it. Mama always said eyes told the truth even when mouths were lying.

But Sarah nodded. William had to think she believed him. "Thank you."

William held up the book. "I brought Dickens for us."

Stories by the British author Charles Dickens were Sarah's favorite. But today, her mind was on other things. "I can't stay. I must go watch for Mr. Fenn's boat."

On the way back to the house, something in the grass caught Sarah's eye. A dagger-shaped hawk feather, striped brown and white. Mama had always loved the hawks that soared above the fields. Sarah picked up the feather and tucked it into her pocket.

When she went inside and climbed back up to the roof, a schooner was rounding the bend from the Sassafras River. Mr. Fenn was on his way to buy slaves.

Sarah knew what happened to slaves who were sold south. She'd seen them chained in a line for the long journey to Alabama or Louisiana, where they'd be worked almost to death in the cotton fields.

Jesse was too small for that, and too spirited. He'd already seen more than his share of beatings for sassing the overseer.

Sarah looked up and blinked away tears. "What should I do, Mama?" she whispered. Mama's body was buried back by the sycamores, but Sarah figured her spirit was up in that bluebird sky. Right then, a hawk soared over the trees. It circled long and slow over the tobacco field.

Sarah sucked in her breath. She pulled the feather from her pocket.

When slaves whispered about freedom, Mama used to tell Sarah not to listen. Sarah's pa had run away a long time ago, when she and Jesse were small. His plan had been to escape north and then work to buy his family's

freedom. Mama promised he'd come back for them. So even when there was talk of a house nearby in Odessa, Delaware, where folks might help runaways, Mama said it was safer to stay and wait.

But Pa hadn't come. Sometimes, Sarah wondered if he'd ever made it to freedom.

Maybe this feather was a sign. The world was changing. When Mama was alive, it looked as though they'd all be together at the Bradley plantation forever. But with the shift from tobacco to wheat and many more slaves being sold south, there was no promise of that. Maybe Mama was telling her things had to be different now.

The schooner's sail flapped in the wind. It was coming.

Sarah looked up at the hawk. It circled once more, then soared over the trees toward the river.

Sarah tucked the feather into her pocket and stumbled down the ladder. She ran to the slave quarters, plunged her hand into a straw mattress, and pulled out the cloth sack that held Mama's vegetable money. She'd earned it by selling extra green beans and potatoes she grew in their small garden by the slave quarters. It wasn't much, but it was all Mama had left them.

Next, Sarah crept into the plantation's empty kitchen. She filled a burlap sack with dried beef and bread, a small jug of water, and a sharp knife.

Then she raced for the stables and burst in the door. "Jesse!"

Old Mabel whinnied. Jesse startled so much he dropped the brush he'd been using to groom her. "What is it?"

"Come with me!" Sarah grabbed Jesse's hand and fled for the prize house by the water.

Jesse's old brown hat flew off as they raced by the kitchen. He tried to stop, but Sarah tugged his arm and kept running.

"Leave it! We have to go!"

It was her only chance to save him.

Chapter 2

HIDE-AND-SEEK

"Ready?" Sadie leaned against a tree and covered her eyes with her hands. "One . . . two . . . three . . ."

Luke raced into the woods at the edge of their yard. Last time he'd played hide-and-seek with his sister, Sadie, and their friends Zeeshan and Noreen, it was Noreen who found the best hiding spot. Luke ducked behind a big boulder.

"Ready or not, here I come!" Sadie called.

Luke crouched in the dirt and waited. He heard Noreen squeal and laugh. Sadie must have found her right away. A few minutes later, Zeeshan cried, "Aw, man!" Luke was the lone survivor.

"Want to play, Ranger?" Sadie's voice drifted through the trees. Luke peeked out from behind his rock and saw Sadie kneeling next to their golden retriever in the yard, waving Luke's baseball cap in front of the dog's nose. "Find Luke!" she said. "*Find* him!"

Find!

Ranger wagged his tail and sniffed the air. He was *very* good at finding.

Ranger had taken a search-and-rescue dog course with Luke and Dad to learn how to find people who were lost. Ranger could smell something that belonged to a person and then find that scent in the air or on the ground. He could follow the smell to wherever the person was, even if there were other scents swirling

around. Ranger could pick out the person smell every time.

Today, there were lots of smells in the air. Tree smells. Dirt smells. Neighbor-dog smells, and meat smells from the deck, where Dad and Mr. Tarar were cooking kebabs on the grill.

And *there*! There was the Luke smell!

Ranger took off, sniffing. He bounded through the trees, found Luke, and licked him on the ear.

"No fair!" Luke stood up.

Sadie laughed. "Good boy, Ranger!" She and Noreen bent down to scratch Ranger behind his ears.

Ranger loved ear scratches. He leaned into Sadie's hand until a new smell in the air caught his attention.

Squirrel!

Ranger took off again. He raced after the squirrel until it scampered up a pine tree. The squirrel sat on a high branch, chattering down at Ranger.

"Too bad, Ranger," Zeeshan said. "Squirrels are faster than Luke."

Ranger knew that. He chased squirrels all the time but had never caught one. Ranger loved chasing them, though. He loved their furry smells and their swooshy, twitchy tails.

The only bad thing about squirrels was that you weren't allowed to be an official search-and-rescue dog if you couldn't help yourself from chasing them. So even though Ranger had gone through all the training, he'd never passed his test.

That was okay. Now he could play hide-and-seek *and* chase squirrels.

"Kids! Time for dinner!" Mr. Tarar called.

Luke, Sadie, Zeeshan, and Noreen ran to the picnic table. Ranger went into the house through the dog door to get a drink from his water bowl.

As Ranger lapped his water, he heard a faint humming sound from his bed in the mudroom.

Ranger knew that sound. He'd heard it before, coming from an old metal first aid kit he'd dug up in the garden. Once, the metal box had hummed when a boy named Sam and his family were getting ready to go on a long, dangerous journey. Another time, it made the sound when a boy named Marcus needed help in a big arena far away.

Now the box was humming again.

Ranger went to his dog bed and nuzzled his blanket aside. There was the first aid kit. Beside it sat a quilt square that Sam had given Ranger and a funny-shaped leaf Marcus had tucked under his collar when they said good-bye.

Those things were quiet. But the first aid kit hummed louder and louder.

Ranger pushed the kit's leather strap with his nose until he got it over his head, so the box hung around his neck. Soon, the humming filled the whole mudroom. Light began to spill from the cracks in the old metal box, and it grew warmer.

Ranger's skin prickled under his fur. He felt like he was being squeezed through a hole in the sky.

The light got brighter and brighter. *Too bright!* Ranger squeezed his eyes closed until the humming stopped and the hot metal cooled.

When he opened them, he was standing in a garden next to a big brick house.

Ranger sniffed the air. It didn't smell of

cool autumn leaves and kebabs like the yard at home. This air was warmer and wetter. It smelled of river water and horses and sweat.

Luke and Sadie and their friends weren't here. But there were two men standing on a dusty path. One wore a dark vest with shiny metal buttons. His voice was angry.

"I'm offering good money for these slaves, and you've *lost* one of them?" He picked up a tattered hat from the ground and shook it in the air. "Where in the devil has he gone?"

A man with a thick mustache answered, "I'm so sorry, Mr. Fenn. He can't have gone far. We'll call in the dogs if we have to, and we'll find him. We will find him in no time at all."

Chapter 3

THE PRIZE HOUSE

Find!

Ranger's ears perked up. He trotted up to the men and sniffed the dusty hat.

The man in the vest yanked it away. "Get out of here, dog!" He turned to the other man. "Don't you have bloodhounds?"

"I'll send for them," the man said.

Ranger tried to sniff the hat again. The man holding it swatted him away.

Didn't they want him to find someone? When Ranger found a person in the woods at training, Luke always petted him and hugged him and said, "Good job, boy!" Then Ranger had a drink of water and they went home.

Home.

These men didn't look like they'd be good at petting. But maybe if Ranger found the hat person, he'd get to go home.

He backed away from the men and sniffed the air. *There!* Amid the smells of horses and river and dirt, Ranger caught the scent of the hat person. He followed it away from the house, past a field of strong-smelling plants, and along a trail by the water.

The air was full of smells.

Bird!

River!

Deer!

And there! Hat person! Ranger followed the scent to a small wooden box of a building. He jumped up and pushed the door with his paws.

When the door swung open, a girl inside gasped and backed away.

Ranger sniffed in her direction. She was not the hat person. But he could tell the hat person was nearby. Ranger wagged his tail to show the girl that he was friendly, but she stumbled and tripped over the handle of a big wooden machine.

Ranger sniffed the air inside the shed. He could smell the strange plants and the girl, mice and wood and . . . *there!* Ranger tracked the hat-person smell to a big barrel in the corner. He sat down next to it, and barked.

"Shhh! Please!" The girl started crying.

Ranger stopped barking. He'd found the hat person and given the alert. But the person didn't come out and pet him like Luke would have. And now the girl seemed even more afraid.

"Who's there?" a gruff voice called from outside.

Sarah sucked in her breath. But then she saw Old Isaac in the doorway. He was a bear of a man whose arms bulged with muscles.

"Isaac!" Sarah ran to him. "We need your help! Master Bradley's fixin' to sell Jesse. We gotta leave right away!"

Jesse's muffled voice came from the barrel. "You didn't tell me nothin' about that!"

Isaac stared at the barrel. Then he looked back at Sarah with sad eyes. "You can't run, child. You won't make it."

"But he's not strong enough to pick cotton. You know that!" Sarah grabbed Isaac's arm. She could already hear the bloodhounds yelping up by the house. "And you know his temper. If he ends up with a different master . . . Please! We'll hide in barrels. You can load us onto the boat with the rest."

Isaac shook his head. "You ain't got a prayer if I send you off with the tobacco." He started to pry open Jesse's barrel.

"No!" Sarah cried. But the lid came off.

Jesse crawled out and looked up at Sarah, his eyes fierce. "Why didn't you tell me they was planning to sell me? How do you even know that?"

Sarah was crying too hard to answer.

Ranger stepped up to Sarah and licked her hand. She pulled it away.

Isaac frowned. "Where'd the dog come from?"

"I don't know. But please . . ." Sarah's voice shook. "Hide us. If they sell Jesse south, he'll never survive. They've already sent out the dogs."

Old Isaac pressed his lips together tight. He closed his eyes and took a long, slow breath. When he opened them, he said, "Listen to me. If you're set on leaving, you do it this way." He

led them outside the prize house and nodded toward a thick grove of trees and bushes by the shore. "On the other side of those trees, there's an old rowboat all beached up in the cattails. Take it across the creek and get yourself good and hidden. Once it's dark, you can row on up the Sassafras River until it gets too shallow. From there, you can walk to Odessa. Word is, you'll come to a brick house with a lantern lit in the window, and you'll find help there." Isaac looked up toward the big house. "I'll do what I can to give you time."

"Thank you." Sarah felt like her chest might explode. She grabbed Jesse's arm and tugged him through the brush.

Ranger followed them at a distance. Everything about this place made his fur prickle. The strange smells. The running and hiding and whispering. How was he supposed to help?

"I ain't doin' this!" Jesse said, and pushed away from Sarah.

Sarah wanted to scream, but she forced her voice to stay even. "Jesse, you heard what I told Isaac. They're selling you south. Today!"

Jesse folded his arms. "You don't know that. You can't —"

Ranger raced ahead of them and barked. Sometimes that stopped Luke and Sadie from arguing and made them laugh. But these children only looked more frightened.

Sarah's heart jumped into her throat, but then she realized that this shaggy yellow dog was nothing like the bloodhounds. It wagged its tail, bounded up to Jesse, and licked his face.

Jesse laughed, and the way his eyes crinkled reminded Ranger of Luke. Ranger licked the boy's cheek again and nuzzled his hand.

Sarah could hear the other dogs barking up

near the house. It wouldn't be long before they got here, too. "Jesse, please! We *have* to go."

Jesse's lower lip quivered, but he jutted out his chin. "I don't have to do nothin'." He stayed by the dog, stroking its head.

Sarah wanted to pick Jesse up, throw him over her shoulder, and run. But she couldn't. And all he seemed to care about now was this fool dog.

"How about . . . What if we take the dog?" she said quietly.

Jesse looked up. He looked at the dog. "Fine."

Relief flooded over her. "Come on!" They plowed through the brush and found the rowboat. Sarah pushed it into the water and held it steady while Jesse climbed aboard. He pulled the dog in beside him.

Then Sarah took a deep breath, stepped into the boat, and pushed off.

Chapter 4

ACROSS THE CREEK

Sarah pulled hard on the oars, but the water felt as thick as molasses. The wind was against them, and the oars kept getting stuck in the water plants.

"What's this?" Jesse lifted the old first aid kit from around Ranger's neck and opened it. "Bandages and stuff."

"Put it in the bag with our supplies." Sarah nodded toward the burlap sack. She wished she'd thought to bring some medicine, too. What if one of them got hurt or sick? Sarah's hands already burned with blisters.

Finally, the rowboat bumped against shore on the other side of the creek. Sarah jumped into the shallow water and held it while Jesse and Ranger climbed out. Ranger shook the water from his fur. Sarah and Jesse tugged the boat into the weeds at the edge of the water and flipped it upside down.

Sarah pulled the kitchen knife from her sack. She found a sumac tree at the edge of the woods and hacked at a thick, leafy branch until it came free. She dragged it through the high grass and draped it over the rowboat. Four more branches, and the boat was disguised as a stubby sumac.

Sarah wiped her brow with her sleeve. "Come on. We'll hide in the trees until dark."

Just as Jesse stood up, Ranger growled, quiet and low. He jumped up on Jesse, who stumbled back to the ground.

"Hey!"

Jesse started to stand, but Sarah whispered, "Shh! Wait!" She dropped to the ground and crept forward through the weeds. Cold mud soaked through her dress, but she stayed low.

"See anything?" a man's deep voice called.

"Nothin'," another man said. "I reckon they set out on foot. The dogs'll have 'em soon."

A boat came into view through the weeds. Fast and silent, Sarah slipped back to Jesse. She lifted the edge of their rowboat and motioned for him to crawl underneath. Sarah followed him and made a noise to call the dog. But it didn't come; it just stood alert in the grass, staring out toward the creek.

They were out of time. Sarah lowered the boat, and the world went dark. She huddled close to Jesse in the musty river-mud air and prayed that dog wouldn't draw the men in to search.

• • •

Ranger's ears pricked up. He waited, listening. Soon, the men's angry, impatient voices floated through the brush again.

"Nothin' but trouble."

". . . hard worker . . . good with the horses . . . a bold and active fellow . . ."

". . . whip some obedience into that boy."

The girl and the boy were afraid of these men. Ranger could tell. He trotted down the creek bank to draw the men's attention away from the hidden rowboat. Away from the children.

When the men's boat drifted into view, Ranger barked.

The man from the house — the one with the big mustache — was rowing. When Ranger barked, he looked up, then pulled harder on

his oars. His boat glided past the hidden rowboat in the weeds. The men didn't even glance
at the funny-shaped sumac. They were looking at Ranger.

"It's that mutt from the house. Musta
swum across the creek," the man with the
shiny-button vest said. He was still holding
that dirty old hat that belonged to the boy.

"Too bad he's not a bloodhound," the man
with the mustache said. He pulled a silver
flask from his pocket and drank from it.

The other man looked down at the hat in
his hands. He held it out toward Ranger. "How
'bout it, mutt . . . you gonna find this boy for
us?" He leaned over so far the boat tipped. He
shook the hat again. "Go on . . . find that slave!"

Find?

Ranger loved finding when Dad or Luke
gave the command. But the children were

afraid of these men. These men were not kind like Dad and Luke.

Ranger kept his tail still. He backed off from the boy's hat and looked away.

"Worthless mutt!"

Across the creek, the bloodhounds let out a chorus of wild barks. The man with the vest squinted over the water. "You reckon they got 'em?"

"Maybe so!" the other man said. He turned the boat around, and they headed back toward the prize house on the other side of the creek.

When the men were gone, Ranger pawed at the upside-down rowboat.

Sarah lifted an edge and peeked out. "They're gone," she whispered. She and Jesse crawled out from under the boat. Sarah pulled a strip of dried beef from her sack, tore it in half, and gave some to Jesse.

He bit into it and tore off a piece for Ranger. "You want some, dog?"

Ranger wagged his tail, and Jesse tossed him the scrap of meat. It wasn't juicy like Mr. Tarar's kebabs. It was tough and chewy and salty. But it was still meat, and meat was good.

Sarah and Jesse stayed close to the boat as the sun sank lower and lower. Finally, it slipped away into the trees, and the sky faded from twilight to dusk. Somewhere in the woods, a wolf howled, and Sarah shivered.

But nothing out there scared her as much as the men back at the plantation.

Chapter 5

NORTH AT NIGHTFALL

When night fell, Sarah started rowing again.

The blisters on her hands had burst long ago, but she couldn't stop. Not until they got to Odessa and found the brick house Isaac had talked about, with the lantern.

There was nothing for Ranger to find now, so he sat beside Sarah while she rowed. Once, she slowed down little by little until the boat stopped. When Ranger looked up, her eyes were closed. He licked her hand. She jumped and started rowing again.

After a few hours, the rowboat got stuck

in the mud. No matter how hard Sarah pulled the oars, it didn't move. She grabbed her sack and climbed out into the mucky water. Jesse and Ranger followed her.

"Where we goin' now?" Jesse asked.

Sarah pointed into the trees that hung over the narrowing river. "We'll follow the river until it ends, then look for the road to Odessa," she said, sloshing through the murky water. She wished it were deeper, deep enough to carry them all the way to Philadelphia and freedom. But she'd dusted the frame of Master Bradley's big map in the library often enough to know that the river that led there was the Delaware, miles to the east.

Thick mud threatened to suck Sarah's shoes from her feet, but she pushed on.

Jesse sighed and stopped to wipe his sleeve across his brow. "How much farther is it?" His voice was high and whiny. Even though he was

only three years younger than Sarah, sometimes she felt like his mother. With Mama
gone, she was the closest he had.

"We're close," Sarah said, even though she
doubted it was true. She grabbed Jesse by the
hand. "Come on." His damp fingers kept slip-
ping out of hers, but she tugged him along as
best she could. It was only a matter of time
before he got too tired, too hungry, to travel
anymore.

As the hours went by, swamp gave way to
woods. Finally, the trees thinned out. Farm-
houses dotted the roadside.

"Is this Odessa?" Jesse forgot to keep his
voice low.

"Shhh! I think so," Sarah whispered.

They walked past dark houses, all through
the sleeping village.

"I don't see no lantern," Jesse whispered.

No matter how hard they looked, how

fiercely Sarah hoped, the houses of Odessa stayed dark. Jesse stopped in front of an ivy-covered brick church, lit in a sliver of moonlight.

"How 'bout here?" he said. "Ain't churches supposed to help people? They always sayin' love thy neighbor."

Sarah hesitated. She had heard stories about runaway slaves getting help at Quaker meetinghouses.

But when Master Bradley brought Reverend Hayworth to give a sermon on the plantation, he preached how slaves ought to obey their masters. He said those who didn't would see the wrath of God along with the overseer's whip. "Just 'cause it's a church don't mean they count us as neighbors," she told Jesse.

"Then where we gonna go?" Jesse's voice trembled. Sarah knew it wouldn't be long before he refused to go anywhere.

"I'm not sure." Sarah reached into her pocket and felt the feather, but Mama wasn't sending her any answers. She looked east, toward the horizon. The sky was getting lighter. Wolves howled, calling to one another in the distance. "But we can't be here when the sun comes up." She took Jesse's hand and pulled him away from the church, into the woods at the edge of town until she found a sheltered spot. "We have to hide. It's going to be light soon."

"I hate this!" Jesse wrenched his hand away from her. "We never shoulda left!" He stomped off through the trees.

Ranger started to follow him, but Jesse whirled around and swatted him away, "Get outta here, dog! I don't need either of you!"

Fine, Sarah thought. *Go on.* Jesse was always running off when he was angry, but Sarah knew it wouldn't be long before he came back to her, looking for beef jerky and company. Why couldn't he *listen*?

Sarah flopped down and leaned against a tall pine tree. She took out a piece of bread and bit into it. The crumbs were stale and dry in her mouth. She swallowed hard and looked down at the dog. "Want some?" She held out the last bit of bread.

Ranger sniffed. Careful not to nip her fingers, he took the bread in his mouth. It was nothing like the warm, soft bread Luke and Sadie's mom made. But Ranger was hungry, and the home bread wasn't here.

As the sky grew light, Sarah grew more and more worried that Jesse might go back to that church on his own. She took a shaky breath and stood up. "We better find him before he does something foolish."

Find! Finally, Ranger could help. He followed

Sarah through the woods. Jesse's scent trail was fresh and strong.

When the trail opened up to an empty clearing, Sarah looked around and sighed. Then she headed off down the path that led back into town.

Ranger barked. Jesse hadn't gone that way. His scent trail led the other way, through thicker brush. Ranger started in that direction. He barked for Sarah to come, but she didn't.

Sometimes, in search-and-rescue training, Ranger ran ahead of Luke or Dad and found the hidden person all by himself. When he got there, he barked and barked — that was the alert — and then Luke or Dad came and found the person, too.

Jesse wasn't far away, Ranger could tell. He'd find Jesse and bark until Sarah came.

Ranger followed Jesse's scent through more trees and along a stream. The scent grew stronger. Jesse was close.

Ranger started to run, but then the wind shifted. Ranger stopped and sniffed the air.

Jesse's scent was still there, with a mix of new smells that made the hair on Ranger's neck stand up.

Deer.

Blood.

And wolves.

Chapter 6

THE SCENT OF WOLVES

Ranger stood, sniffing the air. He'd caught the scent of wolf once before, when he went camping in a big wild park with Luke and Sadie's family. That wolf had been howling from far, far away, but something about its smell had still made Ranger whimper in the tent.

This wolf smell was stronger. It wasn't the smell of one wolf — it was the smell of a pack. And they were close.

Ranger wished Dad or Luke were here. When Ranger was practicing outside and his trainers or handlers thought something ahead might be dangerous, they shouted, "Ranger, wait!" and then sometimes, "Ranger, back!"

Ranger wanted to go back.

But the Jesse smell was strong, too. Ranger started through the trees. Soon, he came to a clearing and sniffed the air.

There! In the tall grass!

Seven wolves crouched around the carcass of a deer, snouts buried in its open belly, tearing at the fresh meat.

Where was Jesse?

Ranger dipped his head and crouched low to the ground. Slowly, he followed Jesse's scent trail around the edge of the clearing, and then —

Crack!

Ranger pricked up his ears. The wolves stopped eating and stared toward the trees.

They hadn't smelled Ranger. Their yellow

eyes were fixed on the boy who had fallen when the tree branch broke.

Jesse.

He was sprawled in the weeds, so close. But Ranger couldn't run to him, or the wolves would attack them both.

For now, the wind was still blowing the wolves' smell his way. They hadn't picked up his scent.

A deerfly buzzed in Ranger's ear, but he didn't shake his head or flick his tail. He didn't even blink.

The largest wolf, a female with silver fur and black-tipped ears, stood up. She lifted her head, sniffed the air, and growled low in her throat. Ranger didn't move.

Neither did Jesse. Ranger could only see the top of the boy's quiet, dark head through the weeds.

The female wolf sniffed the air once more. She turned back to the deer in the grass, lowered her head, and started tearing at it again. The other wolves did the same.

The big female had seen Jesse, Ranger knew. She had breathed in his smell, sized him up, and decided he was no threat. But another dog so close to the wolves' kill would be a different story.

Ranger stayed low. Paw by quiet paw, he crept forward until he was close enough to nudge Jesse's ankle with his snout.

Jesse sucked in his breath. "Dog!" he whispered.

Ranger turned. He led Jesse back into the thicker trees. When the wolves' scent was mostly gone, Ranger stopped. Jesse dropped to the ground, crying. He wrapped his arms around Ranger's neck and held on for a long time.

"Jesse!" Sarah came rushing through the trees. She grabbed Jesse and hugged him, then pushed him away. "I was worried to pieces!"

"I'm sorry," Jesse said, wiping his nose with his sleeve. He looked up at her with big, shining eyes. "I'll stay right with you from now on. Wherever we go."

Sarah looked up at the sun. "We can't go anywhere until dark. Let's find a place to rest."

They chose a spot where the pine needles made a soft blanket under some trees. Jesse stretched out and closed his eyes. Soon he was asleep.

Sarah sat down and leaned against a tree. Ranger curled up beside her. She reached out and stroked his neck. "You think we'll make it to freedom, dog?"

Ranger knew she was talking to him, and that she understood he wouldn't answer. Luke did that sometimes, too, especially when he was sad or worried.

"I hope I did the right thing. Making Jesse run." Sarah pulled the hawk feather from her pocket. A tear rolled down her cheek, and she reached up to wipe it away. Ranger licked her hand, then settled back down and flopped his paw over her foot.

"I couldn't let Jesse go south. He never would have survived. But then I started thinkin' . . . if I get him to freedom, I'm gonna be free, too." Sarah twirled the feather in her fingers. "I always dreamed about that, dog. I told Mama once, and she slapped my hand so hard it stung all afternoon. She said I had no business thinking such thoughts. But I kept thinking them anyway."

Sarah sighed. "William Bradley always promised he'd take care of me — like that should be all I'd ever dream of." She looked down at Ranger. "I guess it takes somebody who's never been another person's property to believe that's any kind of dream."

• • •

Sarah dozed through the afternoon. She dreamed of feathers that lifted her into the sky, of crystal-blue rivers that carried her north to freedom. When she woke, the air was cooler. The sky was almost dark, but she could still see that dream river in her mind. It reminded her of the waters on Master Bradley's map in the library. The wide, winding Delaware River that flowed all the way north to Philadelphia. Pennsylvania was a free state.

She nudged Jesse awake. "Come on . . . it's time to go."

When they got to the trail that led back into Odessa, Sarah went the other way.

Jesse stopped. "Where you goin'? We gotta find that house with the lantern."

"No, we don't," Sarah whispered. She looked up and pointed to a star. "That's the North Star, Jesse. If we keep it to our left, we'll be traveling east, toward the Delaware River. It leads to Philadelphia . . . where we can be free."

Even in the dim moonlight, Sarah could see the uncertainty in Jesse's eyes. "We don't even got a boat."

"We don't need a boat. We only need the river." She took Jesse's hand, but she didn't pull him. He had to believe in her. "We'll walk along the shore, all the way to Pennsylvania."

Jesse looked up at her. "And then we'll be free?"

Sarah nodded. "I promise."

Chapter 7

FREE INDEED?

Sarah and Jesse walked through the trees with Ranger at their side. After a long while — Sarah couldn't tell how much time had passed — she heard the rush of water. They turned north and followed the river until the sun came up, painting the water purple-pink.

"You sure this river's gonna lead us to Philadelphia?" Jessie asked, yawning.

Sarah nodded. "But not just yet." She motioned Jesse into the trees. "We need to hide until it's dark again. Try to rest."

"I'm hungry," Jesse said. Their dried beef

and bread from the plantation were long gone. Sarah searched around and found a handful of berries. Long ago, Mama had taught her about the berries in Mrs. Bradley's gardens and the nearby woods, so Sarah knew which were good to eat. These weren't quite ripe, but they were safe, and she was afraid to go far. She ate one, puckering at the taste, and handed the rest to Jesse.

He tasted one and scrunched up his face. "These don't taste like the berries Mama used to pick for us."

"No. They need more sunshine." Sarah sighed and smiled a little. "But Mama would want you to eat them to stay strong. She'd be proud of you, you know, coming all this way."

"You think?" Jesse stared at the puffy clouds rolling through the sky. Then he looked back at Sarah. "I figure she's probably watching over us somehow."

"I figure that, too." Sarah nodded at the berries in his hand. "Finish those and get some rest."

Jesse ate the rest of the berries, then sprawled out under a drooping pine branch. Sarah crept in beside him and hugged her knees to her chest. She tried to stay awake, but the sun got warm and her eyes grew heavy. Soon, she was asleep.

Ranger sat close to them all day. He was hungry and thirsty. Twice, red squirrels went racing past with their bushy tails flying behind them. But Ranger knew his job wasn't done.

When the sun went down and the air cooled, Ranger nuzzled Sarah's ankle. She sat up and shook Jesse awake. "Get up. It's time to go."

That night, Sarah guessed they made twenty miles before the sun came up and it was time to hide again.

But the next night was blustery and stormy. They couldn't travel as quickly. Sarah and Jesse slogged across swollen creeks, holding tight to each other's hands. Ranger stayed close beside them and never slowed down, even though his paws were sore and thick with mud. Once, a tree limb came crashing down and nearly landed on Jesse. And the river was raging wild. Sarah was afraid to get too close to the bank.

Finally, the rain stopped. The sky was starting to brighten when they came to a road. Sarah and Jesse watched from the trees as carts and carriages rolled by. Some carried fancy-dressed men and women. Others hauled wagons of potatoes and carrots and greens. One held a crate filled with squawking chickens.

A boy who looked about Sarah's age pulled a wagon loaded with newspapers. One blew off the pile in a gust of wind, and when the boy was gone, Sarah chased it down.

"Jesse, look!" She held up the newspaper and pointed to the biggest letters at the top of the page.

"You know I can't read," he said.

"I'll teach you. When we find a place to live. It says *Pennsylvania Freeman*. And see this?" She pointed to a line of smaller print and whispered, "Philadelphia."

"We made it?" Jesse's eyes were huge.

Sarah nodded. "We must be near a market. Follow me."

They kept to the edge of the road until there were no more trees. By then, they could hide in the crowd.

Sarah took a deep breath and pulled Jesse into a sea of all kinds of people — brown faces and black faces and pink faces all going about their day together. There were men in top hats and women in long dresses. Sarah looked down at her own dress, brown with river mud. They shouldn't have to hide anymore, but they needed to look like free black people who had every right to be walking through the market. How would they blend in looking such a fright?

Sarah didn't know where to start. She'd have to find work here, and a place for her and Jesse to stay. But where? Her eyes burned with tears. What if she'd made Jesse a promise she couldn't keep?

"Are you lost?" A girl a little older than Sarah stepped up to them. Her faded blue dress was worn but clean. She held a basket with bread and greens and something wrapped in brown paper.

Ranger sniffed at it. Fish.

"Yes," said Jesse. "And hungry, too. We —"

Sarah cut him off. "We're fine." Her heart thudded in her chest. Maybe this girl was a

former slave, too, or a free black who would help them. But it was hard to know who to trust.

The girl nodded, then reached into her basket, broke off a piece of bread, and held it out. Jesse grabbed it before Sarah could stop him. He took a big bite and chewed, crumbs spilling down his dusty shirt.

The girl reached down and stroked Ranger's head while her eyes took in Jesse's torn pants, Sarah's muddy dress and shoes. Finally, they met Sarah's eyes. "You're fugitives," the girl whispered.

Sarah nodded, her heart pounding. She was afraid, but she couldn't keep her promise to Jesse without help. "I have money. Can you help us find a place to stay?" Sarah whispered.

The girl looked around nervously. "I think so," she said. "There's a church nearby."

Jesse narrowed his eyes. "Sarah says just 'cause someplace is a church don't mean they count us as neighbors."

"That's quite true. But this church will." The girl took off without saying anything more, weaving her way through the market. Sarah and Jesse followed her along one street. Then she seemed to change her mind. She ducked out of the crowd and led them down a quieter alley.

The girl kept looking over her shoulder. It made Sarah feel jumpy. If Pennsylvania was a free state, why was the girl scared? She led them to a building made of bricks and stone.

An inscription above the door caught Sarah's eye.

If the Son, therefore, shall make you free, ye shall be free indeed.

Was it true? Pennsylvania was a free state, but everything still felt hurried and heart-pounding and dangerous. Sarah looked at the girl with the basket. Tears burned her eyes again. "Are we safe now?"

"Shhh! Hurry!" The girl opened the door and motioned urgently for them to get inside. "The sad truth is, none of us are safe with all the slave hunters around," she said as they stepped into the cool darkness of the church. "Wait here." She motioned to a bench, set down her basket, and disappeared through a doorway.

Sarah's stomach ached from worry. She reached into her pocket and felt the feather's soft edges. *Keep us safe, Mama*, she prayed. *Let the words over the door be true.*

Ranger settled next to Jesse, and the boy scratched behind Ranger's ear. No one scratched like Luke, though. Ranger missed his home family. He missed cookouts and hide-and-seek and —

Horses!

Ranger's ears pricked up. He trotted to the door. It was closed, but Ranger could hear sounds coming through the cracks.

Horse hooves. A whinny. A man's angry voice.

Ranger barked.

"Shh!" Sarah hissed at him from the bench.

Then the basket girl came running in with a tall, plump woman beside her.

"This way, children!" The woman motioned them toward a door. "There's slave catchers outside. Come with me!"

Chapter 8

SLAVE CATCHERS

Sarah jumped up, grabbed Jesse's arm, and pulled him down the aisle. Her burlap sack thumped against her side as they raced into another room and down a shadowy set of stairs. The woman slid open a door that led into a dark space. Sarah couldn't see how big the room was or how far it went.

"Follow this tunnel," the woman whispered. "You'll find yourself in another basement. Wait there and keep quiet, no matter what. Someone will come for you when it's safe." She hurried them into the tunnel, and the light vanished as the door scraped closed behind them.

Sarah felt the dog's cool nose on her ankle and heard Jesse's voice behind her.

"I can't see nothin'," he whispered.

"It's all right. Put your hand on my shoulder." Sarah crept forward. She kept one hand on the stone wall, feeling her way. Every few steps, she stopped to listen, but the tunnel was quiet except for Jesse's breathing beside her and the dog's toenails clicking on the stone floor.

Finally, the passage opened up into a room. "This must be the other basement," Sarah whispered. She felt her way around the cool walls and found a door on the far side. She wanted to open it, but she was afraid of who might be out there. And the woman at the church had said to wait. "They'll come for us when the slave catchers are gone."

She heard Jesse sigh and felt his arm slip

away as he slumped down onto the floor. "What if the slave catchers don't go away?" His voice was quiet. "What if nobody comes for us ever?"

"They will," Sarah said. She sat down beside Jesse. "Someone will come." She put her arm around him like Mama would have, and tried to convince herself that her words were true.

It was hard to tell how much time passed in the dark. Finally, there were footsteps.

"You all right in there?" a voice called.

The door opened and light spilled into the room. When Sarah's eyes adjusted, she saw a wiry, thin old woman with silver hair swept into a bun. She was no slave catcher.

"We're all right," Sarah whispered.

"Follow me." Without another word, the woman whirled around and hurried up a set of stairs just beyond the door. Sarah, Jesse, and Ranger followed her. They passed through a kitchen with a warm fireplace. The air smelled of soup. Sarah longed to stop, to eat and rest, but they raced through the room and out the back door to an alley behind the house.

"Wait!" The woman's eyes darted up and down the buildings. When she seemed satisfied, she took off again toward the street corner.

Sarah stayed with the woman and pulled Jesse along behind her, but she was hungry and exhausted and ready to cry. What good was getting to a free state if the slave catchers followed you there? "Where are we going?"

"And who are you anyway?" Jesse blurted.

The woman didn't stop or even turn to look at them. "You can call me Miss Mary. I have a room above my cake shop where you'll stay until we can move you on to safety."

"Move us?" Jesse said. "Ain't Pennsylvania free?"

Finally, the woman stopped walking and turned to look at him. "Philadelphia is crawling with slave catchers. And your master's got broadsides all over town." She pulled a paper from her pocket and unfolded it.

RUNAWAY FROM THE SUBSCRIBER
60 DOLLAR REWARD!

Negroes **SARAH** and **JESSE** escaped from the Bradley Plantation on the 21st of April 1850. Sarah is about twelve years of age with smooth brown skin, much freckled, just over five feet tall. Had on when she left a dress of homespun blue. Jesse is about nine years of age, a cunning boy with a fine round face, brown skin, about four and one half feet tall, wearing work trousers and shirt. A reward of sixty dollars will be paid for their apprehension and security.

~JONATHAN BRADLEY

Sarah's heart sank. "Then where can we go?"

Miss Mary started down the street again. "Mr. Still and others are at work on a plan to move you north."

"North . . . to Canada?" Sarah whispered. She'd heard slaves whispering about Canada as if it were some land from a long-ago story. She liked imagining her pa there. But she'd also heard Master Bradley's warnings, that Canada was a real place, with winds so cold a runaway would freeze to death in a night.

"We shall see." Miss Mary stopped at a small brick building with a blue awning. She pushed open a bright red door, and a bell rang. A boy in his teens looked up from behind a case full of pastries. Jesse's eyes went big. He pressed his face against the glass until Sarah pulled him back. But she couldn't resist reading the names of the sugar-brushed treats on display — gingerbread, apple tart, plum cake, quince pie. Her mouth watered.

Ranger sniffed the air and wagged his tail. This place smelled like the cupcake shop where Luke and Sadie went after school sometimes. Maybe that meant he was getting closer to home.

The old woman pointed to a staircase down

the hall. "Go on upstairs. You'll find a room with a window to your right." She looked them over. "I'll bring some water so you can clean up. Then we'll get you supper."

Supper. Just the word made Sarah's stomach growl. She wanted to hug the woman, but Miss Mary didn't seem like the hugging kind. "Thank you," Sarah said, and started up the stairs.

"Before you go!" Miss Mary called. Sarah and Jesse looked back at her. "If you hear this" — She picked up a wooden spoon from the counter and banged it against one of the pots that hung from the ceiling. An awful clanging sound rattled the whole house — "it means there's trouble and you must go out your window and hide on the roof."

Sarah's stomach twisted. "Is that safe?"

"No," the old woman said. "But you'll hold tight to the shingles and do your best. It will be safer than staying if the slave catchers come."

Chapter 9

SOUND THE ALARM!

Miss Mary brought Sarah and Jesse water she'd heated over the fire and left them to scrub three states' worth of dirt from their hands and faces.

Soon after, she returned with bowls of hot stew, hunks of bread, and two slices of buttery yellow cake.

"This is the best thing I ever ate," Jesse said as he mopped up the broth with his bread, then took a big bite of cake. When he was done, he sprawled out on the mattress and was snoring before Sarah had even finished her stew.

Sarah gave her almost-empty bowl to Ranger, then lay down beside Jesse and drifted to sleep. She dreamed of Canada and fire alarms . . . clanging bells that wouldn't stop.

When Sarah opened her eyes, the bells were still clanging. She remembered Miss Mary's warning — slave catchers! — and shook Jesse awake. "Get up!"

He grumbled and rolled over, so Ranger tried to help. He pawed at Jesse's shoulder while Sarah flew to the window and pushed it open.

There were voices downstairs. At least two men. Maybe three.

Sarah leaned out the window and tried to see where Miss Mary meant for them to go. The window was in a dormer — a bit of house that stuck out from the rest. The roof slanted down from its peak on both sides. Right outside the window, there was the narrowest of ledges, barely wide enough for Sarah's foot. If she climbed out now and something happened to her, Jesse would be captured for sure. He'd have to go first, she decided.

"Jesse," she said, trying to keep the fear out of her voice. "You need to climb up to the roof."

"I ain't goin' out there." Jesse's eyes were huge.

Ranger could tell Sarah was afraid of the men downstairs. Now he could feel the vibrations of their footsteps, coming closer. Ranger nudged Jesse toward the window.

"Go!" Sarah said. "I'll be right behind you."

Jesse climbed out and balanced on the ledge. Sarah could hear the men coming upstairs — their gruff voices and Miss Mary's quiet one. A door opened down the hallway. Miss Mary's calm voice grew louder.

"Don't know why you think that. My only help in the shop is Albert downstairs."

A door slammed. The footsteps came closer.

Sarah held her breath. A different door creaked open. Theirs would be next.

She ran to the window and leaned out.

"Up here," Jesse whispered from above.

"Hold on tight. I'm coming." Sarah lifted one leg over the windowsill.

"Really, gentlemen. Must we continue this?" Miss Mary's voice was louder than it needed to be for the men beside her in the hallway to hear. Sarah could tell it was meant as a warning.

She took a deep breath and swung her other leg over the windowsill, hanging on so tight splinters dug into her fingers.

"Come on," Jesse whispered from atop the dormer.

Sarah was starting to climb when the door to their bedroom creaked open. She swung the window shut as she scrambled up onto the roof.

Inside, the dog started barking. Sarah hoped it would drown out the sound of her movement as she crawled over the shingles. They were rough under her hands, warm from the day's sun. When she reached Jesse, she crouched beside him to catch her breath.

• • •

Ranger stood between the door and the window. Three men stood around Miss Mary — a tall one with a torn, dirty vest; a medium-size one with a thick beard; and a short, round, bald one.

"Well, what do we have here?" The bearded man swaggered into the room. Ranger barked. He lifted his lip to show his teeth and growled.

"Easy there, mutt."

Ranger growled again, low in his throat.

The man didn't come closer, but he turned to Miss Mary. "You best call off your dog unless you want trouble."

Miss Mary smiled up at him. "Sadly, this dog belongs to my brother, who's gone on a trip to New York. Dog won't listen to anyone but Joseph."

Ranger barked again.

The tall man nudged the one with the beard. "Check the closet."

The other man stepped toward the closet. Ranger leaped forward, barking at him, and the man jumped back.

Miss Mary stepped up and flung open the closet door. There was a pile of old blankets stacked inside. "Are you satisfied?"

The tall man started toward the window, but Ranger barked again and lunged at him. The man stopped, then turned to Miss Mary.

"All right. But if you see them, you know where to find us."

Miss Mary led the men out of the room. Ranger listened to their footsteps on the stairs and finally heard their horses ride off down the cobblestoned street.

"You are a fine dog," Miss Mary said when she came back. She pushed open the window and whispered up, "They're gone." A moment later, Sarah and Jesse climbed back inside, and Jesse collapsed on the mattress.

"Thank you," Sarah said, wiping sweat from her forehead.

"Your dog deserves thanks." Miss Mary nodded toward Ranger. "I do believe he would have torn the limbs off anyone who came near that window."

Sarah knelt down and stroked Ranger's head. "Good dog. Thank you."

"Get some rest. There's no telling what

morning will bring." Miss Mary looked out the window, her forehead full of worry lines. She gave them a blanket from the closet.

When Miss Mary left, Sarah petted Ranger a little longer. Then she climbed onto the mattress beside Jesse. She kept listening for the awful clanging sound. But all she heard was Jesse's breathing. Eventually, hers slowed to match it.

Ranger circled on the wood floor and curled up beside the mattress. He'd done a good job. Sarah said so. But the first aid kit in Sarah's sack was still and quiet. His work must not be done yet. When would he get to go home?

Chapter 10

SECRETS AND STEAMBOATS

In the morning, Miss Mary hurried Sarah and Jesse down the street to a brick house with a carriage outside. A man named William Still put a few coins in Sarah's hand. He said it would buy them passage on a steamboat to travel up Lake Champlain.

"You will find work in Vermont," Mr. Still promised.

"Is it safe there?" Sarah asked.

"Safer than here. The slave catchers can only earn so much money bringing you in. It's hardly worth their time to be chasing you up into the mountains."

The man holding the horse's reins shifted in his seat. "We must be off."

"Mr. Brown will take you to Whitehall, New York, where you'll board the steamboat," Mr. Still said, handing Sarah some papers. "If anyone stops you along the way, show these documents."

"How's that gonna help us?" Jesse asked.

"They're forged freedom papers," Mr. Still said. "They say you were freed when your owner passed away."

Sarah nodded and tucked the papers in her sack. She and Jesse climbed up into the carriage, and Jesse slapped his knees. "Come on, dog!"

Ranger jumped into the carriage and curled up at Jesse's feet.

When the wheels started rolling, Sarah reached into her pocket and touched the feather. *Thank you, Mama.* They weren't free yet. But every mile between them and the slave catchers helped.

• • •

Ranger slept most of the first day, even though the road was bumpy. That night, they stayed at a roadside tavern. Mr. Brown got a room with a bed upstairs. Ranger and the children slept in the barn with the chickens.

The next morning they set out again. Every time they passed through a town, Sarah watched for slave catchers and held her breath. But no one even asked to see their papers.

When they reached Albany, the carriage stopped at a boxy brick house. A man named Mr. Myers came out to meet them.

"Captain Sherman is expecting you. We've sent word to the Robinsons as well. They own a farm in Vermont. It's safe there, and they always need good workers." He fed Sarah and Jesse and Mr. Brown and sent them on their way.

The journey took four days in all. When they arrived at the dock in Whitehall and saw the steamboat waiting, Sarah's eyes filled with tears of relief. She thanked Mr. Brown for the carriage ride, handed over her coins, and climbed aboard the enormous boat with Jesse.

Ranger trotted along after them until a crew member stepped in front of him. "Whose dog is this?"

Sarah turned, and her heart sank. Jesse would scream and shout all the way to Vermont if that dog got left behind. "He's ours, sir," she called to the crew member. "He's no trouble at all. I promise."

"It's a full voyage," the man said, shaking his head. "We can't have extra cargo."

"He ain't cargo!" Jesse shouted, and ran to Ranger's side.

Sarah started after him, but then a finely dressed man with a scruffy beard stepped between them. "What's this now? Do we have a stowaway?"

Sarah held her breath, waiting for Jesse to have his fit and get them thrown off the boat.

But when Jesse spoke, his voice was quiet and careful. "He a real good dog, sir. Very well behaved. Better than me, oftentimes."

"Is that so?" the man's voice boomed but his eyes twinkled. "I suppose it won't do to leave him behind." He turned to the crew member. "Let them be. And get back to work."

The crew member nodded. "Yes, Captain."

"Captain?" The word flew from Sarah's mouth.

The man nodded. "Indeed. I'm Captain Sherman. And you are?"

Sarah's throat was too dry to answer. Her first instinct was to reach for the forged papers. But then she remembered the man from Albany had sent word to this steamboat captain. He was expecting them. He meant to help them. "My name is Sarah." She curtsied. "And my brother is Jesse."

Captain Sherman nodded. "Welcome aboard the *Burlington*. Have you ever seen such a fine vessel?"

Sarah shook her head. She'd never seen anything close. "It's beautiful."

"Mr. Dickens thought so, too."

Sarah's mouth dropped open. "Mr. . . . Charles Dickens?" she whispered.

"You know his writings?" Captain Sherman looked surprised. "He rode with us some years back and wrote about the voyage in a magazine. He called my boat 'a perfectly exquisite achievement of neatness, elegance, and order.' I like the sound of that, don't you?"

Sarah nodded. She managed not to cry until the captain left her for his wheelhouse.

Then she leaned against the rail and looked out over the water. Tears streamed down, cool on her cheeks in the lake wind. It seemed impossible to imagine. Just over a week ago, she'd been someone's property, about to see her brother sold south and not a thing she could do to stop it. Now she was a passenger on this fine boat, a boat that Mr. Charles Dickens had called "a perfectly exquisite achievement of neatness, elegance, and order."

Jesse found a bench and fell asleep with Ranger at his side. But Sarah stayed at the railing long after the captain steered his boat away from the dock. She looked over the water and whispered the words to herself. *Neatness, elegance, and order.* That was what their new life would be like.

But there was still a journey between her and Jesse and that new life. Many more miles of lake. A long walk to a farm where no one knew them. Sarah looked at the sunset spilling reddish light over the mountains. Could you wish on a pretty sky the way you wished on a star?

It was worth trying. She stared into the pink-apple sky and let her heart fill with hope. *When we get to Vermont,* she thought, *let the people on the farm be as kind as Captain Sherman. Let us find work and be safe. Let our new life begin.*

Chapter 11

CHANGES IN THE AIR

When Sarah and Jesse stepped off the steam-boat in Vermont, a man with a long face and a dark jacket pointed at them. "There!"

Sarah felt her blood go cold. *No! Not here! Not now!*

They couldn't have come all this way only to have slave catchers waiting to grab them before they even got to the farm. Sarah clutched Jesse's hand and looked for someplace to run, but the man was already blocking her way.

"Mr. Myers sent word that you would be coming." He held out a hand with long, bony fingers. Sarah stared at the hand and tried to make sense of it all.

Mr. Myers sent word . . .

Could this man be from the farm Mr. Myers spoke of, here to meet them? That would mean their journey was over. It felt like too much to hope for, but Sarah forced herself to speak. "Are you Mr. Robinson?"

"Indeed I am."

Ranger stepped up and sniffed the man's hand. He smelled like damp earth and hard work. And something else, too — the wool sweater Luke's grandmother made him. The man scratched Ranger behind the ear, then lifted his hand toward Sarah again.

Finally, she understood that he meant for her to shake it. "I'm sorry," she said, reaching out to him. "It's been a mighty long trip."

The man nodded. "I can only imagine. But

that journey has ended now. We have jobs for you if you're good workers."

"We are, sir," Jesse said. "I'm real good with animals." He looked at Sarah. "We both are."

"Excellent," said Mr. Robinson. "We can use more hands with our sheep." He looked down at Ranger. "And a good farm dog is always welcome, too. So let us be off."

• • •

When they arrived at the farm, there was hot stew and a cozy room above the kitchen. Ranger slept in the barn with the other animals but came bounding out to meet Sarah and Jesse the next morning.

A farmhand named Amos was right behind him. "Ready to work?" Amos walked Sarah and Jesse through the yard, under black walnut and honey locust trees, telling his story along the way. Amos had been a slave once, too, only he hadn't run away like Sarah and Jesse. His owner in Virginia had died and freed Amos in his will.

"I came north and been working here ever since." Amos stepped up to a place where a rocky stream ran through the trees. It was dammed up to make a pool. "Here's where we wash the sheep to get 'em ready for shearing." He turned to Ranger. "You want to help me bring them over, dog? Come on!" He ran toward the sheep and turned back, slapping his knees for Ranger to come, too.

Ranger wagged his tail and bounded off. He raced all around the sheep and nudged them where Amos wanted them to go. Ranger liked helping with the sheep. He loved their musty, wet-sweater smell and the way they ran when he chased them through the damp

morning meadow. It was almost as much fun as chasing squirrels.

After Ranger drove the sheep to the pool, Sarah and Jesse helped Amos and some other men hold and wash them. It was hard work, but different from the old work. By the end of the first day, the farm felt more like home than the Bradley Plantation had in all of Sarah's years there.

Sarah and Jesse settled into routines: helping with the sheep, tending cattle, picking rocks from the new field. Each week, they were paid a wage, and each week, Sarah tucked the coins into Mama's pouch. It was her and Jesse's someday money, for a home of their own.

The summer days slipped by, one after another. Ranger chased sheep and ran after rabbits with the other farm dogs, until the days began to shorten and new smells crept into the air. Falling leaves and pumpkins.

The farm was a fine place, but Ranger couldn't understand why he was still there. Sarah and Jesse were safe, weren't they? When would he get to go home?

• • •

On a late September morning when the air smelled of wood smoke and apples, Amos stopped Sarah on her way to the barn. "Mr. Robinson wants to see you."

Sarah felt as if her shoes were made of iron as she walked toward the house. She felt a flash of panic she hadn't felt in months. "Have I done something wrong?"

"You ain't heard the news?" Amos held open the door for her. "Congress went and passed a new Fugitive Slave Act."

"Didn't they already have one?" Sarah didn't hear much of what happened in the nation's capital, but she knew there was a fugitive slave law from way back before she was born. It said fugitive slaves could be returned to their owners, even if they ran away to free states. "I thought Vermont just up and ignored that law."

"That's the old law. This new one's something else." Sarah followed Amos into the warm kitchen. Mr. Robinson's wife was filling candle molds with beeswax. The days were already getting shorter.

Mr. Robinson stood in the study with a paper in his hand. He nodded to Amos, who hurried back outside. Then Mr. Robinson turned to Sarah. "Amos told you of the new law?"

Sarah nodded.

"Sadly, our nation now requires citizens to assist with the return of fugitive slaves. There are harsh penalties for those who do not. Even in northern states like Vermont."

Sarah's heart jumped right up into her throat.

She looked out the window, half expecting to see the slave catchers there. But it was only Jesse in the meadow. He was hugging a great big sheep so another farmhand could stamp a dark blue letter *R* on its rump in case it ran off to a different farm and had to be returned.

Sarah swallowed hard. "Does that mean we can't stay?"

Mr. Robinson shifted his weight from one foot to the other. "The only truly safe place for a fugitive now is on free soil farther north. In good faith, I must recommend that you leave as soon as possible." He handed her a small purse with some coins. "Here are your wages and a bit more for your journey."

"Journey *how*?" Sarah blurted. She'd thought all the journeying was over — all the running and hiding and looking over her shoulder.

"I've sent word to a man named Noadiah Moore, who lives just this side of the border in

Champlain, New York. He owns a lumber mill in Canada. He has helped us find work for fugitives before."

"In Canada?" Sarah whispered. It still sounded like a make-believe place.

Mr. Robinson nodded. "You can take McNeil's Ferry across the lake whenever you're ready. I am in contact with Stephen Keese Smith in Peru, New York. He's with the Clinton County Anti-Slavery Society. He will meet you and take you to Mr. Moore."

Sarah swallowed hard and looked out the window. There was Jesse, working with Amos to wrangle another sheep. Jesse needed a life like this. He could never go back to the plantation. Neither could she.

Sarah turned back to Mr. Robinson. "Thank you, sir." She held up the sack of coins. "For this and for your kindness. We will leave in the morning."

Chapter 12

UNDER THE BARN

Amos took Sarah and Jesse in a cart to the ferry dock in the next town and said good-bye. "I'll be thinking of you," he promised.

Sarah handed over some coins and climbed onto the boat with Jesse. She had thought he'd have one of his angry fits when she told him they had to leave the farm. But he didn't. He asked why, then listened while she told him about the new Fugitive Slave Act. He never said another word about leaving, but Sarah watched his expression go from shocked, to sad, to tired and resigned.

Now, Jesse leaned against the rail and stared back at shore. Sarah put her sack down and stood beside him, petting Ranger with one hand, waving with the other until Amos got so small they couldn't see him anymore.

"This is the strangest boat I ever seen," Jesse said when he finally turned away from the railing.

Sarah had to agree. There were six horses on the deck — a team of three yoked together on each side of the boat. They were walking on a track that moved with them, so no matter how many steps they took, they didn't move forward. "Poor horses," Sarah said, blinking away tears. "It's awful walking and walking and never getting where you want to be."

"That's where you're wrong." A crew member who must have overheard their conversation winked at Sarah and pointed to the moving track. "That's connected to a paddle wheel in the water. The horses are turning it as they walk, so they're making progress just fine, ferrying themselves and all the rest of us across the lake."

Sarah nodded and tried to smile. She still wondered if she and Jesse would ever find their way to a real home.

Ranger didn't care much for the horses. They looked bored and surly, and it was hard to go anywhere on the deck without walking behind them. Ranger didn't want to get kicked, so he stayed close to Jesse until the boat arrived on the New York side of the lake.

"Now what?" Jesse held Ranger's collar and looked up at Sarah.

"Now . . . now we find Mr. Smith." Sarah tried to sound more confident than she felt as she stepped off the rocking boat onto land.

"You've found him," a man said quietly, taking Sarah by the arm. "I'm Stephen Keese

Smith. Mr. Robinson sent word by telegraph that you would be arriving. Come quickly."

Sarah and Jesse followed the man up the hill to a waiting horse and carriage.

"I'm sorry to rush you so," the man said as he gestured to the carriage. "But it is difficult to know when one is among friends."

Once again, everything happened so fast, it left Sarah's heart pounding with anxiety. There was a too-fast, bumpy carriage ride through the trees. When they arrived at the farm, Mr. Smith drove the carriage behind the house. He jumped down and looked all around, then motioned for Sarah and Jesse to follow him.

Barn swallows swooped over them as they ran across the grass to the barn. Ranger came, too. The barn was full of smells — chickens and pigs, horses and cows, animal feed and wet hay and manure. He breathed it in and pawed at some straw on the floor.

"This way!" Mr. Smith hurried them through the barn to a water trough against the back wall. Behind it, bales of straw were stacked higher than Sarah could reach. Mr. Smith pulled the trough away from the wall and tugged at one of the bales. When it slid away from the wall, it left a hole — a dark, open space that didn't end where the wall should have been. "You should be safe here," Mr. Smith said.

"We gotta hide here all night?" Jesse's lower lip quivered.

Mr. Smith nodded. "We can't take any chances. New York is a free state, but many here want nothing to do with abolitionists. And with the new law, we must take care to keep your presence secret until Mr. Moore

comes for you in the morning." He bent down and held a lantern to light their way through the tunnel of straw. "My wife will bring you some supper soon."

Sarah took a shaky breath and crouched down to crawl into the dark with Jesse and Ranger behind her. Inside the secret room, it wasn't as dark. They were on the lower level of the barn, but light spilled from cracks in the floorboards over their heads. The walls were all stone, with shreds of spiderwebs hanging in the corners. Cattle tromped over the wood floor above them, and water dripped from the boards.

Mr. Smith went back to the house, but it wasn't long before his wife came out with stew. She set the bowls down without a word, glanced quickly over her shoulder, and dragged the bale back into place, leaving Sarah and Jesse to have supper. They ate almost all of their stew, but both saved a bit in their bowls for Ranger. He lapped all around the bowls' edges until they'd been licked clean.

Night fell, and even the noisy cows above them settled down. When Ranger had sniffed everything there was to sniff in this strange new place, he circled around in the dirt a few times and curled up in a corner to sleep.

Jesse lay down with his head on Ranger's belly and dozed off. Sarah sat leaning against a cool stone wall. She couldn't stop thinking about the worry in Mrs. Smith's quiet eyes. Nothing about this place felt safe.

But in the morning, they'd go to Mr. Moore, and he would take them to Canada and then . . . then what? Sarah fell asleep trying to imagine what a home there might look like. Would it look like the Robinsons' farm?

Sarah dreamed of a free Canada farmhouse, with woodstoves blazing in every cozy room and fuzzy, plump sheep in the meadows.

She woke to the sound of voices in the barn.

Jesse sat up and whispered, "You suppose that's Mrs. Smith with our breakfast already?"

"I don't think so," Sarah answered. It was still dark. The voices were getting louder. They were men. Not just Mr. Smith but two or three others. Maybe more. And they were angry.

Chapter 13

A RACE FOR HELP

Sarah's heart was pounding out of control, so loud she was sure the men would be able to hear. She held a finger to her lips, signaling Jesse to stay quiet, and crept as close to the bale of straw as she dared. The voices were clearer. The men were shouting now.

"Move aside, Stephen!"

"Don't care if we have to burn down this whole barn!"

"We know you got runaways in here!"

Sarah's heart felt as if someone were crushing it in a fist. She looked over at Jesse to see

if he'd heard. He was huddled in the cob-
webby corner, clinging to the dog. His eyes
were wide with terror, and there was nothing she could do to comfort him. They were
trapped.

Sarah pressed her ear to the straw. She
heard Mr. Smith talking, more quietly than
the others. "My friends, you have searched the
whole barn. Unless you believe me to be a wiz-
ard who's turned runaways into chickens, you
can see that you are mistaken."

"Step aside, then!" another man's voice
called, hard and sharp. "Get out of the way
and let us see behind that trough."

Ranger didn't recognize these men's voices,
but he understood they were trouble. At the
dog park, some dogs howled and barked without ever meaning harm. But others growled in
a different tone — territorial and reckless and
fierce. They were the dangerous ones.

Ranger left Jesse and padded quietly to the other wall, where Sarah crouched with her ear pressed to a bale of straw. Ranger listened.

The men kept shouting.

There were animal sounds, too. Nervous pigs and chickens.

Then footsteps, coming closer.

Mr. Smith shouting, "Let me go!"

And close — *too close!* — the scrape of a bale of straw against the stone floor. Sarah jumped back just in time to keep from falling into the main room of the barn as a burly man in a nightshirt pulled the bale away from the wall.

Ranger leaped out at him.

The man startled and fell. Ranger stood over him, barking his toughest bark. He turned and saw another big man holding Mr. Smith with his arms pinned behind him. Ranger ran at that man as fast as he could, jumped up, and thumped his paws against the man's torso. The man stumbled, and Mr. Smith flailed away from him and stood in front of the hidden room.

"Get out!" he yelled at the men. "You've seen there's nothing here but a farm hound. Now go!" His voice was loud and firm, but he was alone. The other men stood together in a pack, and they didn't back away.

Ranger tore out of the barn, barking his loudest bark. He ran around the house, barking up at the windows, and then he raced around the neighbors' houses, making as much noise as he could.

One by one, dark windows lit up. Two neighbor men burst out of their houses. Mrs. Smith came running outside with a lantern. She hurried toward the barn, then stopped and gasped. "Bring help!" she called to the neighbor men. One of them went with her.

The other ran to his horse and rode off down the road.

Ranger stopped barking and galloped back to the barn.

When he got there, Mrs. Smith was standing with the lantern, staring at the three men who'd been shouting. Mr. Smith still blocked the entrance to the secret room.

Ranger went and stood by Mr. Smith. He was trying to talk with the men. "Please, let us be. This is not your concern."

One of the men pulled a bottle from his jacket pocket and took a long swig from it. "It sure is our concern if you're hiding Negroes in there." He lifted the bottle toward the other men, who nodded. "If he won't move out of the way, I say we move him ourselves!" The other men roared in agreement.

"Gentlemen, please . . ." Mrs. Smith began. "Go home to your beds."

"Who's gonna make us?" one of the men said, sneering.

"We are," said a strong voice from the barn door. A new voice.

Ranger saw a shadow in the doorway. Then two shadows, then three and four and five, until the whole entrance was blocked. Men and women streamed into the barn, carrying farm tools — axes and hoes and pitchforks. They surrounded the three men who'd come before.

"The lady has made a fine suggestion," one of the men said quietly. "Go back to your beds."

The three men backed away from Mr. Smith and looked down. They didn't have tails to lower, but Ranger understood that they were submitting. The challenge was over. Sarah and Jesse were safe.

After the men left, Sarah and Jesse came out to the main part of the barn. Mrs. Smith brought food for everyone, and Mr. Smith thanked his neighbors. "How did you know there was trouble?" he asked.

"We didn't," one man said, "until that dog came a-hollerin' and barkin'."

Sarah looked at Ranger. "Thank you, dog."

She looked at Jesse. Her eyes filled with tears of gratitude and relief. Jesse was safe. They were both safe. And when they got to Canada, they would be free.

Chapter 14

A SURPRISE AT THE BORDER

In the morning, a horse and driver arrived at the barn, pulling a cart full of ripe apples. Mr. Smith hauled one crate aside to reveal a false floor in the bottom of the wagon. He lifted a board and helped Sarah and Jesse climb in.

"Thank you." Sarah tried to smile as she settled on the rough boards below. But she was so tired. Tired of hiding and being watchful and moving on. Tired of traveling from one place to the next without ever being free.

"That dog can ride up above," the driver of the apple cart said. "No one's looking for him,

I'd reckon. And the two of you only need to stay hidden until we reach the border. Mr. Moore will meet us there and take you to his property in Canada. He said there's a man who used to work for him . . ." The man looked at Sarah and Jesse thoughtfully, as if he couldn't decide whether to say more. He glanced up at Mr. Smith, who shook his head.

"Best not to get their hopes up," Mr. Smith said.

Jesse popped up from the bottom of the cart. "Get our hopes up about what?"

But Mr. Smith pulled his watch from his pocket and said, "You mustn't delay." He said good-bye to Sarah and Jesse, replaced the floorboard, and moved some apple crates around to hide it. Then the driver tugged at the horse's reins and they were off.

The cart creaked and rumbled and bounced along the road north for a long time. When it finally stopped, Sarah heard men's voices outside. She held her breath, waiting. A crate scraped over the wood above them. Then the wood panel was lifted away, and a man peered down at them. He had thin, wispy brown hair, a boxy chin, and bushy eyebrows that made a worried line across his forehead.

"Are you Mr. Moore?" Sarah whispered.

"I am indeed." The man extended a calloused hand and helped Sarah and Jesse out of the cart. He gestured to a waiting carriage. "I'll take you north from here, to Canada. It's not far, and there is a mill where you can work. There's much to be done at the mill and around the house if you'd like jobs."

"We'd like that very much, sir," Jesse said.

Mr. Moore looked at him for a moment, as if he were studying Jesse's face. Then he said, "Did Mr. Smith mention to you that . . ." He paused. "Perhaps I should wait."

"What is it?" Sarah asked.

"There was a man — a former slave — who worked with us for several years and has since moved on to Montreal. He was a fugitive." Mr. Moore paused again, looking at Jesse's face as if it were a puzzle he could solve. "He said he had family at the Bradley Planation in Maryland and was saving money to buy their freedom."

Jesse's whole face blossomed. "Our pa?" He turned to Sarah. "Did you hear that? He knows Pa!"

Sarah shook her head. "That's not what Mr. Moore said." She was afraid to hope. There had already been so much disappointment, so many hopes that led only to sadness and another journey. "That man could have been anyone," she told Jesse. "Other men did what Pa did."

"That's true," Mr. Moore said. "But . . . may I ask how old you are?"

"I'm nine and Sarah's twelve," Jesse said.

"Remarkable." Mr. Moore shook his head, staring at Sarah and Jesse. "Those are the ages John's children would be now."

Jesse's face fell. "Our pa's name isn't John. It's Jupiter."

"No matter, young man." The apple cart driver stepped forward. "I've carried many fugitives who changed their names when they came north. Makes it more difficult for anyone to track them."

"So that man who worked for Mr. Moore . . . John . . . *might* be our father?" Sarah whispered. The cart driver nodded, and Sarah let herself remember the last time she'd seen her pa. A whispered story told by firelight in the slave quarters. A tight hug. A promise: *I'm coming back for you.*

She had stopped believing in that promise, but now she felt a spark of hope growing in her chest. She looked up at Mr. Moore. "Do you really think it could be our pa? Do you think we could find him?"

"I don't know. Montreal is a big city. But I very much hope so. Either way, you shall have a safe place to work and live in Canada. Shall we go?"

"Don't forget your bag," the man with the cart said. He reached into the compartment in the floor for Sarah's sack. When he pulled it out, some of the contents spilled out among the apple crates. The kitchen knife, a few coins, and off to the side, Ranger's first aid kit.

As Sarah began gathering her things, the old metal box began to hum quietly. Ranger jumped beside it, took the leather strap in his teeth, and tugged the box to the edge of the cart.

"Are you going to carry that to Canada for us, dog?" Sarah scratched him behind his ears.

Ranger leaned into her hand. Sarah loved him, but she didn't need him anymore. Ranger understood that she and Jesse would be all right. And the humming from the old metal box was getting louder.

It was time to go home.

Ranger jumped down from the wagon and licked Jesse's hand. Jesse squatted down. "Did you hear, dog? We're going to Canada now. And our pa is up there somewhere, waiting!"

"We don't know that, Jesse." Sarah couldn't bear the thought of Jesse's hopes being crushed again. "It might not be him."

"Well, I think it is," Jesse whispered, and leaned forward so he and Ranger were nose to nose. "You can come to Canada, too, dog!"

"We should be off," Mr. Moore said, nodding to the carriage.

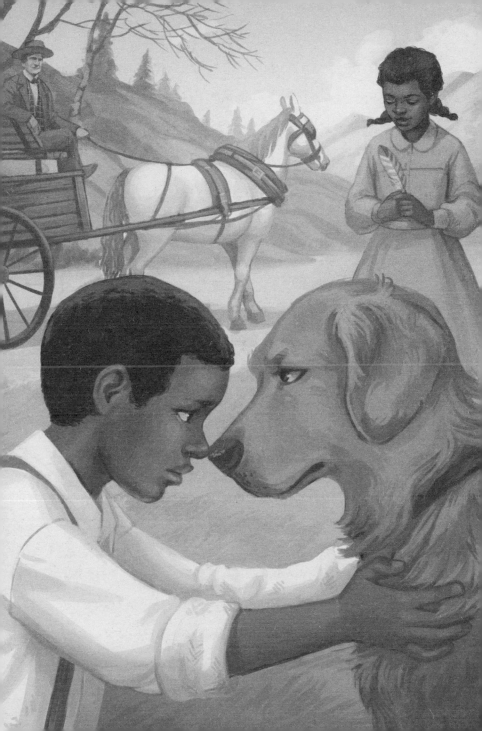

Ranger turned back to the metal box. The humming was louder, even though no one else seemed to hear it.

"Hey!" Jesse called. "You have to come with us!" He turned to Sarah. "Make him come! We can't leave without our dog."

Sarah tipped her head and looked at Ranger. She waited while he nuzzled the strap of the old metal box over his head. Then his brown eyes met hers, and she didn't know why, but she understood somehow that the dog wasn't coming.

"He's not ours," she said quietly. "He gets to choose for himself whether to come or not." She hesitated. "And I reckon maybe he's got somewhere else to be."

Jesse ran to Ranger. "You sure you don't want to come, dog? Even though you're free and all, you could still live with us."

Ranger licked Jesse's cheek. He'd miss this

boy full of so much energy. But he was sure. He'd been missing another boy for a long, long time.

"Thank you, dog." Sarah reached into her pocket and ran a finger over the hawk feather she'd carried all the way from the plantation in Maryland. It had done its job. Mama's spirit had given her the courage she needed to run. After that, she knew, she'd done it herself. She'd led Jesse to freedom.

Sarah leaned forward and tucked the feather under Ranger's collar. "Wherever you're going, this will help you find your way." Then she and Jesse climbed into the carriage. Mr. Moore tugged the horses' reins, and they started off toward Canada. Toward home.

Ranger watched as long as he could.

The humming from the metal box grew so loud he couldn't hear the horses anymore. Light began to spill from the cracks, so bright

Ranger couldn't see the carriage or the northern New York sky. He closed his eyes against the white-hot light.

When he opened them, he saw Luke's face.

"You coming back outside, Ranger? It's time for dinner."

Chapter 15

COMING HOME

Ranger lowered his head and dropped the first aid kit onto the blanket of his dog bed. It wasn't humming anymore.

"Whatcha doing in here?" Luke let the screen door to the mudroom slam behind him. He jogged up to the dog bed and squatted down to scratch Ranger behind his ears. "What's up, boy? Want your water dish outside by the picnic table?"

Ranger leaned into Luke's hand and breathed in his boy's smell — lemonade and woods and fresh soap from washing up for dinner.

"Hey! Looks like you got a feather caught in your collar when we were in the woods." Luke reached for the brown-and-white feather and held it up to the light. "I wonder where this came from. It's too big to be from a robin or sparrow."

Ranger barked. He nuzzled Luke's hand until Luke laughed and put the feather on Ranger's dog bed. "Here you go! I know how you are about your treasures. Just don't let Mom find it. She'll say it's dirty and put it outside."

Luke went to the refrigerator to find more lemonade, and Ranger pawed at his blanket until he found the quilt square the boy Sam had given him at the end of their long journey and the funny leaf from Marcus, the boy from the loud arena with the fighting men and big cats. Carefully, Ranger picked up the feather in his teeth and laid it beside them.

The bird smell on that feather was faint now. Mostly, he could smell Sarah. Ranger breathed in her scent — wood smoke, hidden coins, forest earth, and hope.

He'd helped Sarah and Jesse on their long, long journey. And now, finally, his job was done.

Ranger pawed his blanket to cover the quilt square, the leaf, the feather, and the old metal box. Sarah and Jesse were safe, Ranger could tell. They were home.

"You ready for dinner, boy?" Luke stood grinning with a new cup of lemonade. "Come on outside — everybody's eating at the picnic table, and you know Noreen always drops food. Maybe we can play hide-and-seek afterward. You gotta be on my side this time!"

Ranger barked and followed Luke outside. Home was a wonderful place to be.

AUTHOR'S NOTE

While Sarah and Jesse are fictional charac-
ters, their long, dangerous journey was real
for thousands of fugitive slaves who dared to
escape from their owners in search of freedom. Many of the places in this story were
real stops on what has become known as the
Underground Railroad, a loose network of
friends, relatives, and abolitionists who did
what they could to help fugitives on their
journey north.

Some of the people you met in these
pages — William Still, Stephen Myers, and
the Robinson, Keese, and Smith families —
are also real. While there aren't specific

records of them helping a pair of children like Sarah and Jesse, they were documented anti-slavery activists. The aid they provided to runaway slaves included shelter, food, money, work, transportation, and sometimes even physical protection from slave catchers.

The threat of being sold south to work in a cotton field was a very real one for slaves in 1850. Changes in the economy meant that plantations were growing less tobacco and more wheat, which didn't require as much work. As a result, many plantation owners decided to sell some of their slaves. At the same time, the invention of Eli Whitney's cotton gin, a machine that made cotton much faster to process, had turned cotton into America's leading export. Southern plantations that grew cotton needed more and more workers to keep up with demand. Many brought in more slaves as a result.

The Bradley Plantation is fictional, but it is modeled after the Mount Harmon Plantation in tidewater Maryland, where slaves worked tobacco fields in the eighteenth century. Today, the plantation is open as a museum, and I am grateful to Debbie Brown, who took me on an off-hours tour of the house, including the rooftop porch like the one where Sarah looks out over the water on the day she makes her decision.

And here is another bit of inspiration from Mount Harmon — the feather that I found while walking the grassy trails that led to the water.

Odessa, Delaware, is a real place, and there was reportedly a brick house where fugitive slaves could find shelter. Often, though, slaves who escaped from their owners did so without help. Even those who were promised assistance sometimes found themselves on their own, and this is why I chose to let Sarah and Jesse wander without finding that lantern in Odessa.

The wolves that Jesse and Ranger encounter in the woods are no longer found in Maryland and Delaware, but they were very much a part of the ecosystem there in 1850. How might those wolves have reacted to Jesse and — if they'd smelled him — Ranger? In researching this scene, I spent a morning with Steve Hall of the Adirondack Wildlife Refuge and took a walk with the resident wolves — Cree, Zeebie, and Kiska — to watch and listen as they moved through the woods.

While slave catchers were still a threat to Sarah and Jesse — and to other fugitives who reached Philadelphia — there was also more help available there. William Still was a real-life hero who worked with the Pennsylvania Anti-Slavery Society and kept careful records of the slaves he helped on their way to freedom — more than nine hundred in all. A historical marker stands outside his home on 12th Street in Philadelphia today.

The Mother Bethel AME Church was also a real sanctuary for fugitive slaves and was rumored to have a tunnel during the years this story takes place. Founded in 1794 by a former slave, Richard Allen, the church has been rebuilt several times. It's still on its original street corner, though, making it the oldest church property in the country continuously owned by African Americans.

The *Burlington* was a real steamboat that reportedly carried its share of fugitive slaves up Lake Champlain. New York abolitionist Abel Brown wrote in his memoir, "Many a slave has enjoyed the indescribable pleasure of leaping from the liberty-loving *Burlington* to feel the pleasure of being free."

Some of those fugitives likely ended up at the Robinson farm, called Rokeby, in Ferrisburgh, Vermont. Vermont's constitution outlawed slavery, and the Robinsons were both powerful landowners and fierce abolitionists, so they felt safe having free blacks and former slaves work side by side on their sheep farm. The farm is a museum now and has an excellent exhibit called *Free and Safe: The Underground Railroad in Vermont.*

This is the site of Rokeby's "sheep dip" like the one where Sarah and Jesse worked. The outdoor exhibit includes an illustration showing what the scene might have looked like in the 1800s.

The Fugitive Slave Act of 1850 was devastating to slaves who had escaped north and thought they were safe. It required citizens of northern states to assist in capturing runaway slaves and promised harsh punishments to those who helped fugitives or withheld information. Fugitives who were captured were denied jury trials. Instead, their cases were heard by special commissioners who were paid ten dollars for each case if they sent the accused slave back to his or her master, but only five dollars if they decided the person should remain free. Like Sarah and Jesse, many slaves decided that being "safe" in a northern state was no longer safe enough, so they traveled on to Canada. McNeil's Ferry, which really did run on the power of horses on treadmills, likely carried some of them across Lake Champlain.

Northern New York's population was split on the issue of abolition, but Clinton County had a strong anti-slavery society. Stephen Keese Smith and Noadiah Moore were documented members who likely hid fugitives in their homes, transported them to Canada, and helped them find work. The wonderful North Star Underground Railroad Museum in Ausable Chasm, New York, has collected much of this history and offers bus tours of local sites. I went with them to see the barn where Stephen Keese Smith is believed to have sheltered fugitives.

The barn really does have a secret room in the back, beneath the floor where the cows slept.

Given all of the setbacks and seemingly impossible challenges that fugitive slaves faced on their journey north, it's hard to imagine a hopeful ending like Sarah and Jesse's being a realistic one. The cruel reality is that slavery tore families apart, over and over again. But once in a while, those families found their way back together. In 1850, the same year this story takes place, William Still was working in his Philadelphia anti-slavery office when a former slave named Peter Friedman walked in and asked for help finding his parents, who had come north years before. That man turned out to be William Still's own long-lost brother. You can learn more about their story here: http://www.pbs.org/black-culture/shows/list/underground-railroad/home.

• • •

History is full of stories of helpers who aided fugitive slaves on their way to freedom, but the greater heroes in this chapter of history are the slaves themselves — real-life people who played a huge role in establishing a new nation's economy without getting any of the credit. They were people like Sarah, who held on to feathers of hope in the darkest of times. You can read about them in William Still's own book, *The Underground Railroad: A Record of Facts, Authentic Narrative, Letters, &C., Narrating the Hardships, Hair-breadth Escapes and Death Struggles of the Slaves in Their Efforts of Freedom, as Related by Themselves and Others, or Witnessed by the Author; Together with Sketches of Some of the Largest Stockholders, and Most Liberal Aiders and Advisers, of the Road,* which is available via Project Gutenberg online (http://www.gutenberg.org /ebooks/15263).

I am most appreciative of the following

museums and organizations and their staffs, for providing resources, answering questions, and, in some cases, making special arrangements for me to tour historic sites and collections. If you are interested in the Underground Railroad and the lives of slaves and former slaves, all of these are well worth a visit.

Mother Bethel AME Church in
Philadelphia, PA
https://www.motherbethel.org

Mount Harmon Plantation in Earleville, MD
http://www.mountharmon.org

National Constitution Center in
Philadelphia, PA
http://constitutioncenter.org

North Country Underground Railroad Historical Association and North Star Underground Railroad Museum in Ausable Chasm, NY
http://northcountryundergroundrailroad.com

Rokeby Museum in Ferrisburgh, VT
http://rokeby.org

FURTHER READING

To learn more about slavery, the Underground Railroad, and working dogs, check out the following books:

Aunt Harriet's Underground Railroad in the Sky by Faith Ringgold (Random House, 1995)

Henry's Freedom Box: A True Story from the Underground Railroad by Ellen Levine (Scholastic, 2007)

I Survived the Battle of Gettysburg, 1863 by Lauren Tarshis (Scholastic, 2013)

If You Traveled on the Underground Railroad by Ellen Levine (Scholastic, 1993)

Moses: When Harriet Tubman Led Her People to Freedom by Carole Boston Weatherford (Hyperion, 2006)

Sniffer Dogs: How Dogs (and Their Noses) Save the

World by Nancy Castaldo (Houghton Mifflin Harcourt, 2014)

The Escape of Oney Judge: Martha Washington's Slave Finds Freedom by Emily Arnold McCully (Farrar, Straus and Giroux, 2007)

SOURCES

Many thanks to Dr. Raphael Rogers, EdD, at Clark University for reviewing this manuscript and providing invaluable feedback, and to everyone from the museums and historical sites I visited with my notebook. Your patience, knowledge, and passion are so much appreciated. The following books and articles were also of great help in my research:

Blight, David W., ed. *Passages to Freedom: The Underground Railroad in History and Memory.*

Washington, DC: Smithsonian in Association with the National Underground Railroad Freedom Center, 2004.

Blow, David. "McNeil's Ferry, Charlotte." *Chittenden County Historical Society Bulletin* 4, no. 1, September 1968.

Bordewich, Fergus M. *Bound for Canaan: The Underground Railroad and the War for the Soul of America.* New York: Amistad, 2006.

Brown, C. S. *Memoir of Rev. Abel Brown.* Worcester, MA: printed by author, 1849.

Calarco, Tom. *People of the Underground Railroad: A Biographical Dictionary.* Westport, CT: Greenwood Press, 2008.

———. *Places of the Underground Railroad: A Geographical Guide.* Santa Barbara, CA: Greenwood, 2011.

———. *The Underground Railroad in the Adirondack Region.* Jefferson, NC: McFarland, 2004.

Carbado, Devon W., and Donald Weise. *The Long*

Walk to Freedom: Runaway Slave Narratives. Boston: Beacon Press, 2012.

Franklin, John Hope, and Loren Schweninger. *Runaway Slaves: Rebels on the Plantation.* New York: Oxford University Press, 1999.

Hudson, J. Blaine. *Encyclopedia of the Underground Railroad.* Jefferson, NC: McFarland, 2006.

Pennington, James W. C. *The Fugitive Blacksmith; or, Events in the History of James W. C. Pennington, Pastor of a Presbyterian Church, New York, Formerly a Slave in the State of Maryland, United States.* London: Charles Gilpin, 1849.

Rokeby Museum. *Letters of the Underground Railroad.* Ferrisburgh, VT: Rokeby Museum, 2000.

Ross, Ogden J., Arthur B. Cohn, and J. Kevin Graffagnino. *The Steamboats of Lake Champlain, 1809 to 1930.* Quechee, VT: Vermont Heritage, 1997.

Siebert, Wilbur H. *Vermont's Anti-Slavery and Underground Railroad Record*. Columbus, OH: Spahr and Glenn, 1937.

Still, William. *The Underground Railroad: A Record of Facts, Authentic Narrative, Letters, &C., Narrating the Hardships, Hair-breadth Escapes and Death Struggles of the Slaves in Their Efforts of Freedom, as Related by Themselves and Others, or Witnessed by the Author; Together with Sketches of Some of the Largest Stockholders, and Most Liberal Aiders and Advisers, of the Road*. Philadelphia: printed by author, 1883.

Tobin, Jacqueline L., and Hettie Jones. *From Midnight to Dawn: The Last Tracks of the Underground Railroad*. New York: Doubleday, 2007.

ABOUT THE AUTHOR

Kate Messner is the author of *All the Answers*; *The Brilliant Fall of Gianna Z.*, recipient of the E. B. White Read Aloud Award for Older Readers; *Capture the Flag*, a Crystal Kite Award winner; *Over and Under the Snow*, a *New York Times* Notable Children's Book; and the Ranger in Time and Marty McGuire chapter book series. A former middle-school English teacher, Kate lives on Lake Champlain with her family and loves reading, walking in the woods, and traveling. Visit her online at www.katemessner.com.

DON'T MISS RANGER'S NEXT ADVENTURE!

Ranger goes back in time to join an early twentieth-century expedition to Antarctica, where he befriends a cabin boy traveling with Captain Robert Falcon Scott. They're racing against a rival explorer to reach the South Pole, but with unstable ice, killer whales, and raging blizzards, the journey turns into a race against time . . . and a struggle to stay alive.